Five reasons why you'll love Mirabelle...

Mirabelle is magical and mischievous!

She's full of witchy ideas!

She loves making potions with her travelling potion kit!

Mirabelle loves sprinkling a sparkle of mischief wherever she goes!

She's friendly and fun!

If you could do magic, what spell would you cast?

To make the world fair
for everyone.
– Elise

I would conjure
up huge storms.
– Iris

Deckchairsmasho!
To make furniture smash.
– Alex

A spell to make myself live forever!
– Eben

I would fly in the
sky like a fairy.
– Hazel

To make the whole world
glittery and starry.
– Arianne

Dear reader,

I am delighted to introduce to you to . . .
(magical drum roll please) . . . Mirabelle
Starspell! She is half witch, half fairy,
totally naughty.

Mirabelle lives with her mum, who is a witch,
her dad, who is a fairy, and her brother Wilbur.
She loves casting witchy spells by the light
of the moon, just as much as she likes nature
and fairy magic. In this story, Mirabelle is
absolutely forbidden to bring her witch's wand
and cauldron to the annual fairy get together . . .
but she doesn't always like doing as she's told
. . . in fact, Mirabelle quite enjoys sprinkling a
sparkle of mischief wherever she goes. Besides,
if she did just a teeny, tiny bit of witchy magic,
what could possibly go wrong?!

Mirabelle's family is special, and for any Isadora Moon fans out there, you might even know her already because Mirabelle is Isadora Moon's cousin! Isadora and Mirabelle have had adventures before but this is the first time that Mirabelle will star in her very own story, so make yourself a cup of hot chocolate, settle down, and enjoy *Mirabelle Gets up to Mischief*!

Happy Reading,
Clare Whitston

Senior Commissioning Editor at the home of
Isadora Moon and Mirabelle Starspell

Family Tree

My Mum
Seraphina Starspell

My brother
Wilbur Starspell

My Dad
Alvin Starspell

Me!
Mirabelle Starspell

Violet

Illustrated by Mike Love, based on
original artwork by Harriet Muncaster

OXFORD
UNIVERSITY PRESS

Great Clarendon Street, Oxford OX2 6DP

Oxford University Press is a department of the University of Oxford.
It furthers the University's objective of excellence in research, scholarship, and
education by publishing worldwide. Oxford is a registered trade mark of Oxford
University Press in the UK and in certain other countries

Copyright © Harriet Muncaster 2020

The moral rights of the author/illustrator have been asserted
Database right Oxford University Press (maker)

First published 2020

British Library Cataloguing in Publication Data

Data available

ISBN: 978-0-19-277649-5

1 3 5 7 9 10 8 6 4 2

Printed in China

Paper used in the production of this book is a natural,
recyclable product made from wood grown in sustainable forests.
The manufacturing process conforms to the environmental
regulations of the country of origin.

From the world of ISADORA MOON

MIRABELLE

Gets up to Mischief

Harriet Muncaster

OXFORD
UNIVERSITY PRESS

Chapter ONE

'NO witchy magic!' said Dad, wagging his finger at me. It was Saturday morning and we were all in the dining room together having breakfast. Me, my mum, my dad, and my brother Wilbur.

'Remember,' said Dad, 'this is a fairy celebration, the most important one in the whole year! I don't want to see any of your

witchy things at the midsummer dance tonight. No cauldrons, no potion bottles. No pointy witch or wizard hats!'

'No cauldrons!' I gasped. 'But I always take my travelling potion kit with me, wherever I go!'

'I know,' said Dad. 'And it always seems to cause a lot of mischief.'

'Mischief?' I said trying to look surprised.

'Yes,' said Dad. 'And I don't want any naughtiness at the midsummer's ball this year. You must embrace your fairy side for the night. Why don't you dust off your fairy wand? I never see you using it.'

'That's because it's rubbish!' I complained. 'It only does . . . boring magic.'

Dad raised his eyebrows at me and his fairy wings fluttered in annoyance. I had almost said 'good magic' but stopped myself just in time.

'Dad's right,' chipped in Mum. 'You and Wilbur must embrace your fairy side for the night.' She smiled at us with her dark purple lips. 'You are both half fairy after all.'

Wilbur sighed. He hates being reminded that he's half fairy. He finds it embarrassing and would prefer to be full wizard. I don't mind so much. It can be useful for getting out of trouble. People never expect fairies to be naughty!

'We will *all* do our best to be as "fairy" as possible for Dad,' said

Mum and I stared at her in surprise. Mum is a full blown witch and I could never imagine her trying to be 'fairy,' she loves whisking around on her broomstick and cackling and making potions. Sometimes she can even be quite mischievous too!

'That's settled then!' said Dad. He took a sip of his flower-nectar tea and looked at us all happily over the rim of the mug. Mum crunched down on her spider-sprinkled toast.

I looked back at them and thought about how happy it would make Dad if Wilbur, Mum and I embraced our fairy sides for the night. I decided that I would try my absolute best to be good. No potions, no cauldrons, and no pointed hats!

Chapter TWO

It didn't take me long to get ready that evening. I picked some flowers from the garden to put in my hair, and then I snuck into Mum's dressing room and sprayed

myself with her perfumes until I smelled of marzipan and purple berries. Mum always has the best perfumes. She invents a lot of them herself! Then I went back to my room and rummaged in my toy box until I found my old fairy wand that I never used. It was right at the bottom tangled in some necklaces that my friend Carlotta had given me. Carlotta is my best friend at witch school and we are always plotting and planning things together.

I took the wand and the necklaces out and began to untangle them. I had forgotten all about the necklaces! They both had long silver chains and hanging off each one was a miniature potion bottle.

'They're for when you need to be more secretive,' Carlotta had told me. 'You can take your potions with you wherever you go!'

I stared at the necklaces and my mind began to whir. I knew I had promised Dad that I would only bring my fairy wand to the midsummer dance, but surely it wouldn't hurt to take just a tiny bit of witch magic? He would never know! And it's not like I was planning to *use* the potion bottles. It would just be nice to *have* them. I liked the idea of having a witchy little secret at the midsummer dance.

I started to feel the two sides of me clashing against each other. My fairy side was telling me to leave the potion bottles at home. To just take my fairy wand and to be as good as I possibly could be for Dad. But my witch side was saying the opposite.

And my witch side usually wins.

Five minutes later I found myself running
up the spiral staircase of the tallest
turret in our house. We call it the Witch
Turret and it's where Mum keeps all her
potion ingredients, her spell book and her
cauldron. Mum always has the best, most
expensive and pretty potion ingredients.
Much better than mine! I fancied filling
my tiny bottles with something pretty and
glittering. Something that would look nice
on a necklace. It was only for looks after
all. I wasn't going *use* the potions.

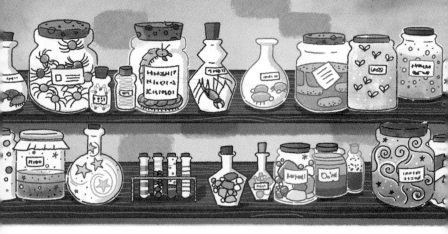

I stared up at the shelves all around the curved walls of the turret room and wondered which ingredients to put in my tiny bottles. There were jars of glimmering mermaid scales, swirling dragon's breath and twinkling star shine. There were strange-looking ointments and tubes of crystals and dried flower petals. Right at the top was a row of jars that were full of creepy crawlies which I never liked looking at because they made me shiver. In the end I pulled down the jar

of dragon's breath and a small
bottle of glittering purple
seeds. I wasn't sure what they
were but they would look pretty in
the tiny potion vials on my necklaces.

By eight o clock we were all ready to go.
Mum had put on a mauve dress and a flower
crown, which looked odd and uncomfortable
on her. Wilbur didn't look happy in his
lavender trousers and flower-pattern shirt.
But Dad was beaming.

'We all look wonderful!' he said. 'Very
fairyish! I'm glad you found your wand,
Mirabelle!'

'Oh yes!' I said, waving it in the air so that a shower of sparks rained down on us all. 'I'm glad I found it too!' Dad looked so pleased that I suddenly felt guilty about the two necklaces that I could feel resting against my chest beneath my dress. But I reminded myself, it wasn't as if I was going to use them.

'Do we have to go?' asked Wilbur as Mum got our broomsticks out of the hall cupboard and I put on my lilac fairy cape made from real flower petals.

'Of course we do!' said Mum. 'It's part of your fairy heritage! You shouldn't be so embarrassed about being half fairy, Wilbur!'

'Being a fairy is a wonderful thing!'
said Dad, puffing his chest out proudly. He
was wearing a smart suit made entirely
from leaves sewn together. He looked very
magical.

'Fairies have an important job to
do on this planet,' he said. 'The biggest
job there is! We do our best to look after
nature. Nature is *so* important.'

'Humph,' said Wilbur, but he looked
a little less embarrassed. Mum handed
us both our broomsticks and we all
made our way out of the front
door. Wilbur and I can

only fly by broomstick,
as we hadn't inherited
Dad's fairy wings.
Sometimes I felt a bit
disappointed about
that. I would have
liked wings!

Mum locked the door and Dad
fluttered up into the air.

'Come on!' he said excitedly as Mum,
Wilbur, and I rose up behind him. 'We
don't want to be late!'

Chapter
THREE

We had to fly quite a long way to the place
where the midsummer dance was to be
held. By the time we got there it was dusk
and I was hungry but I still couldn't help
gasping as Mum, Wilbur, and I circled
above the party on our broomsticks.

A big fire had been lit in the middle of a
clearing in a huge forest and all around it

multicoloured fairy lights had been strung through the trees. There were tables upon tables of delicious fairy food: strawberry cakes, butterscotch biscuits and flower petal sandwiches. My tummy started to rumble. Fairy food is the best!

'Look!' said Dad, pointing. 'There's my sister Cordelia and your Uncle Bartholomew too!' He flew down towards a crowd of fairies and we all followed. I was excited to see my cousin Isadora Moon! Isadora is half fairy like me except her dad, Bartholomew, is a vampire which makes her a vampire fairy.

'Oh good,' said Mum, 'we won't be the only odd ones out tonight!'

'Isadora!' I yelled, landing on the ground with a skid and

giving her a big hug.

'Mirabelle!' said Isadora. She looked pleased to see me and her little bat wings fluttered with excitement. Pink Rabbit bounced up and down beside her and I gave his head a pat. Pink Rabbit used to be Isadora's favourite cuddly toy but her mum magicked him alive with her fairy wand. I always feel a little bit jealous of Pink Rabbit actually. I wish I had my own special pet. Mum has a black cat but he's not very nice. He always hisses at me.

'Let's go and eat some food!' I said. 'Have you seen all the cakes?'

'Yes!' said Isadora. 'But I was waiting for you!' We started to push through the crowd towards the food tables, leaving our parents to chat about boring things.

'Look at those!' said Isadora, pointing to a table that was full of pink spun-sugar clouds, glinting with tiny sugar diamonds.

'Fairyfloss!' I said. 'I love fairyfloss!'

'Me too,' said Isadora.

We each took one and then wandered towards the big fire, both happily munching and talking at the same time. Then we saw a group of young fairies about the same age as us clustered on the grass. They were busy making flower garlands for their hair.

'Let's make one!' said Isadora, so we sat down together and began to twist flowers and leaves into crown shapes. Mine just wouldn't go right. I kept snapping the stems by mistake and the petals kept falling off my flowers. In the end I sighed and threw it down on the grass.

'I'm not good at making flower crowns!' I said.

'I'll help you in a minute,' said Isadora. She had made a beautiful garland that was sitting perfectly on top of her messy hair and now she was busy making a smaller one for Pink Rabbit.

'It's OK,' I said, suddenly feeling a bit bored of flower crowns. My fingers were starting to twitch and I reached inside my dress to feel the two potion bottles that were resting against my chest.

It felt good to have brought a little bit of witch magic with me to this very flowery and fairyish celebration. It made me feel a little bit more like . . . me.

'Isadora,' I whispered, suddenly feeling an urge to be just a tiny bit mischievous. 'Do you want to know a secret?'

'What secret?' asked Isadora, looking up.

I reached into my dress and lifted out the two little potion bottles. They sparkled and glinted in the evening sunlight. Isadora's eyes went big and round.

'Mirabelle!' she said. 'You're not

supposed to bring witch magic to a fairy celebration.'

'I know,' I said. 'But look how pretty the bottles are.'

'What's inside them?' asked Isadora.

'One's dragon's breath,' I said. 'But I don't know about the other. I just found it in my mum's potion room.'

I shook the little bottle so that the sparkly purple seeds tinkled against the glass.

'I wonder what it does . . .' I said, starting to feel intrigued 'Maybe we should go into the woods and find out!'

Isadora shook her head.

'Your witch magic always gets us into trouble!'

'It wouldn't this time.' I said. 'I promise! We could go and experiment in secret. No one would ever know!'

Isadora looked worried.

'I don't think it's a good idea,' she said.

Just then some music started to play and fairies all around us got up and started flittering towards the huge fire.

'The dancing's about to start!' said Isadora, looking relieved. 'We can't miss the dancing! Come on!' she held out her hand for me to take but I shook my head.

'I'll catch up with you in a minute,' I said. 'I need to finish my flower crown. You go! You love dancing!'

Isadora didn't look like she believed me but she got up anyway, took Pink Rabbit's paw and disappeared into the crowd. I stared over at the fire and spotted Mum and Dad beginning to dance. I could just see Mum's black pointed boots poking out from under her pale mauve fairy dress. I knew she would be finding it hard to be 'fairy' for the night too. Especially as she's a full blown witch!

I stayed on the grass for a few minutes, fiddling with my flower crown, trying to resist the overwhelming urge that had just come over me to sneak off into the forest and do a little bit of magic. I had promised myself that I wouldn't do anything with the tiny potions tonight and, more importantly, I had promised Dad that I would be good all night and not do any witchy magic. But the feel of the bottles against my skin was irresistible. I loved experimenting with making potions. It was my favourite thing to do!

I stood up and turned away from the campfire, walking in the opposite direction towards the trees.

'It will be fine,' I told myself as I walked deep into the woods. 'I'll just go and do a little bit of magic on my own. No one will ever know. Dad will never know. And then I'll go and join in with everybody.'

Chapter
FOUR

I kept walking until I got to a dark
and gloomy part of the forest. Then I
stopped. I was all alone. It was perfect. I
knelt down on the ground and took the
necklaces off, admiring again the swirling
and glittering potion ingredients inside
the tiny bottles. I didn't have a cauldron
of course so I took off my shoe and put

it in front of me. Then, before I could change my mind, I poured the little bottle of purple seeds into it, followed by the swirling mist of dragon breath, and stirred them together with a twig. The mixture immediately began to crackle and little stars and moons flashed into the air.

'Ooh,' I whispered and leant closer so that a few petals from my wonky flower crown fell off and drifted downwards. I had no idea what would happen. The mixture began to fizz and hiss. Pink and purple smoke puffed out into the air in glittering clouds, spluttering and crackling as the petals fell into it. I wondered if I should say some magic words but I didn't know what as I didn't have my spell book with me. So instead I just stared down at the mixture, wondering what it would do.

Suddenly the twig in my hand started to twitch and I let go of it in surprise. It landed fully in the potion and began to wriggle. I gazed at it in wonder and then noticed that something else was starting to happen. The flower petals that had fallen into the potion were wiggling about too, rising up and joining together in a rosy clump. The clump began to float around my head, forming itself into a loose dragon-like shape. Excitedly I pulled the flower crown off my head and began to pick off more petals, throwing them into my shoe. As soon as they touched the potion they began to squiggle and writhe, floating up to join the others so that the flower-petal dragon got bigger and bigger. It began to skip and dance around the clearing, flapping its wings.

I looked around me to see what else
I could put into the potion. Leaves! There
were leaves all around! I jumped up and
began to pick them off the trees, throwing
big handfuls of them at my shoe. Any that
touched the potion seemed to come to life,
joining up with other leaves and flowers.
Soon there were five large dragons

made from leaves, flowers
and twigs, rustling
and rippling round
the private little
clearing. I gazed
at them proudly
and then began to
skip with them. We

danced round and round, a whirl of perfumed petals and summer-smelling twigs. I danced until I was out of breath and then threw myself back down on the ground, delighted. I felt as though all the witchy naughtiness had been danced out of me. I was ready to go back to the fairy party now and be good for the rest of the night. I was sure that the dragons would now go off into the forest and no one would ever know about them. They would probably disappear eventually once the spell wore off.

I reached out for my shoe and noticed that it still had a quite a lot of potion left in it. That was odd considering how many things I had put into it but magic is a funny thing. I turned my shoe upside down, trying to shake the potion out of it but it wouldn't budge. I peered in and gasped. Something else was happening now. The mixture had hardened up while we had been dancing. It had shaped itself into a ball. A ball that was starting to grow little arms and legs, a long spiky tail . . . Wings! Claws!

I held my breath as sparks flew and fizzled in the air. The magic finished and something wiggled and snorted in the bottom of my shoe. A tiny purple baby dragon. It was much, much smaller and much more solid than the other dragons as it wasn't made up of wispy leaves and flowers. It had real scales that shimmered in the starlight. It stared up at me with big eyes and then flapped its wings, rising shakily into the air. When it snorted its tiny purple nose, little sparks and clouds of glitter puffed out.

'Hello little dragon,' I whispered and held out my hand. The dragon landed on my palm and began to poke around my fingers. It tickled and I laughed.

'You're so sweet,' I said. 'You need a name!' I thought for a moment, admiring its glittering lilac scales, the same colour as some of the petals that had fallen into the potion.

'Violet!' I said. 'I think it suits you!'

The little dragon puffed out a rose coloured cloud of glitter as though she approved and then flapped off my hand and began to flutter around my body, poking her nose into my long hair before disappearing into the hood of my flowy fairy cape. I smiled, liking the feel of my new little pet snuggled up against my back, and hoped that she wouldn't disappear. Some magic doesn't last and I still had no idea what sort of potion I had made.

Happily I began to make my way back through the trees towards the big clearing in the forest where the fairy celebration was happening. As I walked I wondered what had happened to the other dragons. They had disappeared while I had been distracted by Violet. I expected they had made their way deep into the forest, maybe even becoming one with nature once again.

I could see the flickering flames of the big fire through the trees now and hear

the noise of the fairy celebration.
It sounded louder than before.
There was even the sound of
screaming. Maybe I was missing
out on something exciting?
I walked faster, coming out
through the last of the trees.

Then I stopped.

'Oh my stars,' I gasped.

Above the big flickering fire in the middle of the fairy celebration were my five large dragons circling in the air. Five large dragons made from leaves and flowers and twigs. Their bodies and wings rippled and swirled with dark spaces for their eyes and mouths, which gaped open eerily in the flickering light of the flames. They looked terrifying lit up by the firelight, completely different from the funny, strange dragons that they had seemed to be when I first created them. Fairies were running, flying and screaming in all directions.

'Oh no,' I whispered and put my hand

in my pocket to feel for Violet.

Chapter FIVE

I stared up at the monster dragons and wondered what to do. It was obvious they hadn't been created from fairy magic. Mum and Dad would know it was me! I was going to be in big trouble. My heart started to beat fast and I began to feel a bit sick. I needed to get the dragons away from the party and lure them back into

the forest. But I had no idea how to do it.
The small potion I had made by myself
in the forest had now turned into a very
big mess! I watched in horror as the fire
flickered in all directions beneath the wind
of the flapping dragons. It was getting so
blown about that it looked like it might
even go out. All around me was chaos and
I couldn't see my family
anywhere amongst the
tangle of frightened
fairies. I had no
idea what to do
except stand there
and stare at the
mess I had created.

'Mirabelle!' shouted someone and I glanced over to see my mum running towards me. Her usually neat and perfect fringe was flying all over the place. She looked furious.

'Is this your doing?'

'Umm,' I said and felt myself shrinking into a tiny ball. My mum can be really scary when she's cross. Her dark witch eyes were glinting dangerously.

'I . . .' I began. 'I just wanted to see what would happen if I made a potion with . . . some ingredients that I found.'

'Some ingredients that you *found!*' said Mum, towering over me with her hands on her hips. 'And where exactly did you find these ingredients?'

'Umm,' I gulped.

Just then there was a load more screaming and suddenly we were all plunged into darkness. The fire had gone out. The dragons looked more frightening than ever, silhouetted against the round yellow moon. They were starting to chase the fairies, thinking it was some sort of game.

'Honestly!' said Mum and she reached into her dress and pulled out a necklace just like mine which had ten tiny potion bottles hanging off it.

'Mum!' I said in surprise. 'You're not supposed to bring witch magic with you to a fairy party!'

'I hardly think you can talk!' said Mum but she looked a little sheepish.

'Come with me,' she said. 'Only witch magic will get rid of these monsters.'

I followed Mum back into the forest and we found a quiet place between three large trees. Mum reached into her pocket and pulled out a tiny portable cauldron.

'Mum!' I said again. 'You weren't supposed to . . .'

'I know, I know,' said Mum, waving her hands in the air. 'But it's a good job I did bring my emergency witch kit, isn't it!' she gave me a fierce stare.

'Now which ingredients did you use?' she asked. 'I need to know so I can make a reverse potion.'

'I used some little purple seeds,' I whispered, 'and some . . . dragon's breath. And then I put loads of leaves and things into it too.'

'Hmm,' said Mum. 'Interesting!' She didn't say anything for a moment and I could tell her mind was beginning to whir. Mum loves making potions just as much as me. She and Dad own their own beauty business concocting face creams, perfumes, and lipsticks. She can spend all day up in her Witch Turret experimenting with ingredients. Dad oversees to make sure everything is natural. Together they make a great team.

'I think I know what must have

happened,' said Mum as she placed the tiny doll-size cauldron in front of us. 'But that's not the proper way to make that potion.'

'I know,' I said. 'I'm sorry.'

Mum frowned at me crossly.

'Don't do it again!' she said. 'It can be really dangerous to mix up ingredients when you don't know what they are. And without using a spell book too!'

'I won't,' I said as I watched Mum open up one of the tiny potion bottles, sprinkling a few drops of it into the little cauldron. It immediately began to grow until it was normal size. Mum began to open some of the other bottles and pour more things into the cauldron. A strange liquid that smelt of violets, a pinch of shimmering vanishing dust, a smattering of the same purple seeds. Mum waved her hands above the mixture, her long nails like talons in the moonlight, the colour of blackcurrants. She began to hum, saying words of a spell that I had never heard before. The mixture in the cauldron bubbled and whirled, sending up violet coloured smoke into the air.

'That should do it,' said Mum, peering in at the mixture. 'It's a sort of vanishing potion. We need to sprinkle it on the creatures and they should disappear. They will just become leaves and flowers and twigs once again.'

'Ooh,' I said, peering in too. I always love to watch my Mum make potions. She always looks so magical when she's casting spells. She began to pour the mixture into a couple of enchanted bottles.

'One for you and one for me,' she said. 'We're going to have to fly up on our brooms and somehow sprinkle some of the mixture onto each creature. OK?'

'OK,' I said.

Mum started to pack away, shrinking the cauldron back down to doll size and putting her necklace back on.

'Did any other creatures come out of the potion?' she asked. 'Usually those purple seeds turn into their own thing. If you mixed them with dragon's breath then it makes sense that they may have created a little dragon. Not a leaf or a flower one. A proper one!' She stared hard at me and I felt my face turn red. I looked down at the ground, feeling Violet wriggle in the hood of my cape. I didn't want to put any of the vanishing potion on Violet. I wanted to keep her.

'No other dragons came out of the potion,' I said.

'OK,' said Mum. 'Well I suppose you didn't make it properly anyway.' She stood up and beckoned for me to follow her. 'We had better sort out this mess,' she said.

Chapter SIX

Five minutes later Mum and I were flying
high in the air on our broomsticks, both
clutching a bottle of potion and dodging
fairies who were desperately trying to fly
away from the clearing. I wondered how
we were going to get close enough to the
dragons to throw the mixture onto them.
They were so big and their wings were

beating so hard that a wind was blowing
all around. I shot up into the sky as high
as I could go. Maybe if I could get higher
than the dragons then it would be easier
to pour some of the potion onto them
from above. I soared higher into the air.
Down below the five huge dragons circled,
puffing out clouds of glittering smoke.

'At least they're not blowing fire!' called Mum.

I gripped onto my broomstick tightly with my legs and tried to balance while I opened the lid of the potion bottle. At last I got it open and gripped back onto my broom again with one hand, rocking from side to side in the breeze that the dragons were making with their wings.

'Watch out!' called Mum and I looked down to see one of the dragons starting to fly up towards us. The breeze was getting stronger and Mum was still trying to undo the lid of her potion bottle amongst the chaos of fairies flying all around. There was an almighty gust and I rocketed sideways.

'Help!' called Mum as she was buffeted upside down, dropping her potion bottle.

It began to plummet downwards. I gripped harder onto my broomstick and pointed it towards the ground, shooting towards the bottle, feeling Violet fall out of my cape. But there was no time to catch her. She would be fine. She could fly! I reached out my hand and grabbed the potion bottle just before it fell through one of the dragon's leafy, ripply bodies. I yanked the lid off and sprinkled it onto the dragon's back, immediately flying sideways to avoid being whacked by one of its flapping wings. From a place of safety

I watched as the huge creature began to dismantle itself, the leaves, flowers and twigs dispersing and falling away from each other towards the ground. I had done it! The first dragon had gone!

I looked up and saw Mum hovering in the air high above me. There was no time to fly up and give her the potion bottle back. I would have to use both of them. I whizzed through the air into the space above one of the other dragons and sprinkled some potion onto that one too. Again the huge creature began to fall away, the leaves and flowers raining down onto the ground and onto the heads of any brave fairies who had decided to stay.

I caught sight of Dad, Wilbur and my cousin Isadora staring up through the darkness, gobsmacked. They all had twigs in their hair and Dad looked very cross.

'Mirabelle!' cried Mum, swooping alongside me and holding out her hand for her potion bottle. 'Well done!' She sounded proud despite the fact that I had caused all the chaos in the first place.

Together we managed to sprinkle potion on the last three dragons and the air below us became thick with flower rain. Fairies all around started clapping and cheering. They were no longer running away and some of them had even started to dance, holding out their hands to catch the leaves.

'Thank goodness for that!' said Mum. She patted her fringe back down and then started to reapply her lipstick whilst

hovering in the air on her broomstick.
Then, together we flew down to join Dad,
Wilbur, and Isadora.

Chapter SEVEN

'Wow!' said Wilbur when I landed back down on the ground beside him. 'You were amazing up there, Mirabelle!'

'Thank you,' I said trying not to blush. Wilbur never usually compliments me. Dad was frowning but I could tell he was a tiny bit impressed too.

'What on earth has been going on?'

he asked. Mum looked at me and I gulped. But I had to tell Dad the truth.

'I made a potion using witch magic,' I said. 'And it got a bit . . . out of hand.'

'A *bit!*' exclaimed Dad.

I looked down at my feet. Suddenly I felt really bad.

'I'm sorry, Dad,' I said. 'I didn't mean to ruin your special night. It just all went wrong.'

'I told you not to bring any witch magic to the summer dance!' said Dad. 'You promised you wouldn't!'

'I know,' I said. 'I'm sorry. I promise I'll try to use my fairy wand more!'

Dad sighed and I could see that Mum was looking a little uncomfortable too.

'I know you feel more witch most of the time,' said Dad, 'and that's completely fine. I married a witch after all! There's no need to try and use your fairy wand more—it's important that you feel like you can be yourself. But I was just asking you

to leave the potions at home for *one* night!
You always end up causing mischief with
them!'

'I know,' I said. 'I won't do it again.'

'That's what you always say,' said
Dad. 'No, I think we need another
solution. I've got the perfect
punishment for you.'

'A punishment?'
I gasped.

'Yes,' said Dad.
'It's obvious you need
to learn more about
making potions *properly*
so that you don't keep
getting into messes like

this. I think you need to go and work with Mum in her Witch Turret every day for the next month!'

'What a good idea!' said Mum and her eyes twinkled.

'Really?' I said. This didn't sound like a punishment at all!

'Yes,' said Dad. 'She can teach you to use magic *responsibly.*'

'OK!' I said, trying not to sound too pleased about the idea.

'*And,*' continued Dad, 'you will come and help me in the garden twice a week after your lessons in the turret. It's important to learn about your fairy side too. It's what makes you YOU after all.'

'Oh . . . OK,' I said. Gardening with Dad wouldn't be nearly so exciting as making potions with Mum but I supposed I might learn something interesting. There are some very magical things about being fairy after all. I heard Wilbur snigger next to me and Dad shot him a look.

'You can join in too Wilbur,' he said. 'I know you're more drawn to your wizard side but the fairy side is something to be proud of too. It's what makes you unique!'

'I guess,' said Wilbur and I was surprised that he didn't protest more. Maybe my brother was secretly quite interested in finding out more about his fairy side after all.

'Good,' said Dad. He sounded delighted. 'Shall we enjoy the rest of the party now?'

'I think we should!' said Mum. She put her hand on my shoulder.

'Well done for telling the truth, Mirabelle,' she said. 'I know you caused all this mess but you've done a wonderful job of helping to sort it all out.'

'Oh,' I said and suddenly I remembered something. Something that made me feel guilty all over again.

'Mum, Dad,' I said. 'There's something else I need to tell you.'

'What now?' sighed Dad.

'I . . . um,' I began staring down at the ground. 'I lied to Mum when I said that no other dragons came out of the potion. There was another one.'

'What?' gasped Mum and her eyes flashed dangerously. Her hand reached into her pocket for the bottle where there

was still a little bit of the vanishing potion left.

'Where is it?' she asked, looking around.

'I don't know,' I said, starting to cry. 'She fell out of the hood of my cape while we were flying. But Mum, I don't want you to throw the vanishing potion on her. She's called Violet and she's my pet. I want to keep her!'

Mum frowned.

'I don't know,' she said. 'I'm not sure you deserve to keep her. First you make all this mess by doing potions in secret. And then you lied to me when I specifically asked you about any more dragons!'

'I didn't want to tell you because I knew you wouldn't let me keep her!' I said. Tears began to run down my face and through the watery haze I finally spotted Violet fluttering towards us through the air. I felt sick at the thought of her vanishing.

'I'm really sorry I didn't tell you,' I sobbed. 'And I'm sorry for causing all this mess too. I just really want to keep Violet. I want a pet like Isadora has Pink Rabbit! I promise I'll be good forever if you let me keep her!'

Mum stared disbelievingly at me for a moment and then threw her head back,

cackling with laughter.

'Now Mirabelle,' she said. 'Don't make promises you can't keep.'

'A week then,' I said. 'I'll be good for a whole week. I'll clean out all your cauldrons!'

'Let's make it a month,' said Mum, putting the potion bottle back in her pocket. 'And you can clean out all my bottles and jars too. I suppose Violet is rather sweet.'

We all watched as Violet fluttered near to us and then moved away again, flapping over towards the unlit fire.  She began to blow little purple sparks from her nose. She blew and blew until suddenly the fire burst back into life. But it wasn't just an ordinary fire this time.

It was multicoloured, changing from pink to orange to green to blue. It was a beautiful sight even through the watery haze of my tears. Violet beat her little wings and then flew back over to me, burying her pointed snout into my neck and nuzzling me. Wilbur looked a bit jealous.

'I want a pet!' he said. 'Can I have a dragon?'

'Maybe,' said Mum. 'Let's see how Violet fits into the family first. I don't want any scorch marks on the carpet.'

I looked up at the sky and saw that any fairies who had flown away were starting to come back. They were landing on the ground all around us and starting to dance to the music that was beginning to play. My aunt Cordelia came skipping past and grabbed Dad's hand, pulling him and Mum into the crowd.

Isadora grabbed mine and together we danced round and round the fire, kicking up the petals that lay all over the ground in pretty pink and purple puffs. Even Wilbur joined hands with some of the fairy boys who were nearby and started to dance too. I could tell by the smile on his face that he was truly enjoying himself, giving in completely to his fairy side for the night.

'Mirabelle!' shouted Isadora over the music. 'I can't believe you made all those dragons!'

'I know,' I said, trying not to sound too proud about it.

'You're so naughty!' giggled Isadora and she squeezed my hand fondly. I squeezed back, glad that she hadn't come with me into the forest and got into trouble too.

The party was beginning to look a lot like it had before any of the magic happened. Everyone seemed happy and excited once again and perfumed petals swirled all around. I gazed up at the multicoloured flames and smiled as Violet fluttered in the air above my head. Right now everything was witchy-fairy perfect.

Turn the page
for some
mischievous
things to make
and do!

How to throw a great party!

Who doesn't love a good party?

When planning a party, there's lots to think about, so here's a quick guide on how to get started! You need to ask yourself (and a grown-up!) about the following questions:

1. What **type of party** would you like to have?

2. How many **people** can you invite? And who?

3. **Where** will the party be and what **time** will it be?

4. What **music** would you like?

5. What **decorations** will you need?

6. What **food** would you like to have?

7. Will there be **games?** If so, which ones?

8. Are you going to make or buy the **invitations?**

Once you have answered all of
these questions, it's time to get started!

How to make a fairy drink!

Now that you've worked out what type of party you would like, let's get started on the food and drink. First, let's combine your inner fairy with your inner witch and make your own fairy drink/potion.

Ingredients:

★ 150ml orange juice

★ 150ml berry juice

★ 150ml lemonade

★ A lemon or lime, sliced

★ Ice cubes

★ Edible glitter (optional)

Equipment:
- Measuring jug
- Glasses
- Long spoon
- Paper straw
- A grown-up to help

Method:

1. Put a handful of ice cubes into a jug.

2. Add the orange juice, berry juice and lemonade.

3. Add a few slices of lemon or lime.

4. Add a sprinkle of edible glitter, if using it.

5. Stir the potion in the jug with a long spoon.

6. Pour some into a glass and add a paper straw.

7. Enjoy! Sip slowly to get the full fairy benefits!

How to make fairy cakes

You can't have a fairy party without fairy cakes!
Here's a witch-proof recipe to make tasty fairy cakes!

Ingredients

For the cakes:

★ 150g of unsalted butter

★ 150g of caster sugar

★ 175g of self-raising flour

★ 3 eggs

★ 1 teaspoon vanilla extract

For the buttercream

★ 150g of unsalted butter

★ 250g of icing sugar

★ 1 teaspoon vanilla extract

★ 2 teaspoons hot water

★ Optional edible glitter for decorating the finished cakes

Equipment

- ★ 12-hole cupcake tray
- ★ 12 cupcake cases
- ★ 2 mixing bowls
- ★ 2 metal spoons
- ★ Hand-held electric whisk
- ★ Wooden spoon
- ★ Oven gloves
- ★ Oven
- ★ Small knife
- ★ Piping bag if you have one
- ★ Wire cooling rack
- ★ A grown-up to help

Method:

1. Ask your grown-up helper to turn the oven on to 180°C.

2. Put 12 cupcake cases in the cupcake tray.

3. Put all the cake ingredients into a bowl. Ask your grown-up helper to help you mix the cake mixture with the electric whisk for 1-2 minutes until it is light and creamy.

4. Using the spoons, divide the mixture evenly between the 12 cases.

5. Using the oven gloves, put the tray in the oven and bake the cakes for 18-20 minutes. You will know when they're ready if the sponge bounces back up when you press the top gently with your finger. Make sure you ask a grown-up to help take the tray out of the oven as it will be very hot.

6. Carefully put the cupcakes on a wire rack to cool.

7. Whilst the cakes are cooling, make the buttercream. Put the butter and the icing sugar into a bowl and beat with a wooden spoon until smooth.

8. Add the vanilla extract and hot water and beat again until smooth.

9. With the help of a grown-up, cut out the centre from each cake and cut each scooped-out piece in half to make fairy wings.

10. Spoon or pipe the buttercream into the hole in each cupcake.

11. Place the 'fairy wings' at an angle on top of the buttercream so they look like wings.

12. If using, sprinkle edible glitter over the icing like fairy dust.

How to make fairy flower head garlands

Things to collect:

★ A long piece of vine wire or twine

★ Scissors

★ Flower tape (it sticks to the flowers better than sticky tape)

★ Daisies and other small flowers (cut with permission from a grown-up!)

★ Greenery like ivy or ferns

★ A grown-up to help

Method:

1. Shape the vine wire to the size of your head. Ask a grown-up to cut it just a bit longer than you need, for a bit of wriggle room. Fix it at the right size with floral tape.

2. Wrap some of the greenery around the wire crown. Use the floral tape to hold it in place

3. Group 2-3 little flowers together into small bunches and hold together with floral tape. Make a few little bunches to spread around your crown.

4. Feed each little bunch through the greenery and vine and stick with floral tape.

5. Try it on and decide if you have enough flowers to get the look you want!

6. Keep it in the fridge to keep it fresh until you need to wear it!

Alternative option:
If you'd like your head garland to last a bit longer, you could use different-coloured tissue paper instead of fresh flowers and greenery!

How to make the decorations!

You'll need decorations for you party so here are a couple of suggestions to get you started.

What you need:

★ 10cm strips of paper (in your preferred colours)

★ Glue stick

★ Sticky tape or drawing pins

Method:

1. Sort out your strips of paper into piles according to their colour.

2. Put glue on one end of the first strip of paper.

3. Curve the paper strip into a circle and stick one end to the other.

4. Then put glue on the end of the next strip of paper (a different colour) and then loop it through the first circle and stick it together.

5. Carry on like this, looping each strip through the existing circles, alternating the colours, until you get the length of paper chain that you would like.

6. Put your paper chains up with the help of a grown-up with sticky tape or drawing pins.

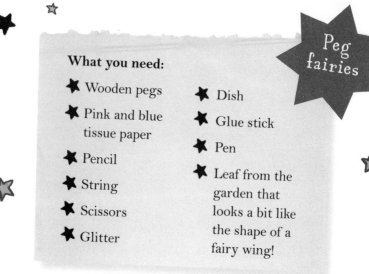

What you need:

- Wooden pegs
- Pink and blue tissue paper
- Pencil
- String
- Scissors
- Glitter
- Dish
- Glue stick
- Pen
- Leaf from the garden that looks a bit like the shape of a fairy wing!

Peg fairies

Method:

1. Place the leaf against the edge of the tissue paper and draw around it with a pencil. Draw as many wings as you need for your fairies. If you want 10 fairies, you'll need 20 wings.

2. Cut out the wings very carefully

3. Now tip the glitter into a dish

4. Use the glue stick to cover a peg in glue.

5. Now roll the peg in the dish of glitter until the peg is well covered.

6. Repeat this for all your pegs.

7. Once the glue and glitter have dried, add a spot of glue on the back of the peg where you want the wings to go and stick two wings onto the peg.

8. Hold it down firmly for about 30 seconds to make sure they stick.

9. Add a little face to the peg head with a pen – two dots for eyes, one dot for a nose and a little smile.

10. If you prefer a different expression, why not get creative! You could have a cross fairy, a happy fairy, a confused fairy and a sad fairy. Think of the games you could play with this crowd of fairies!

11. Hang the fairies up with string to decorate your party room.

How to be a good party host!

- Help your grown-up to get the food and drinks ready.

- Help decorate your party venue.

- When your guests arrive, help them with their coats, show them where the toilets are and offer them a drink. Perhaps they'd like one of your fairy potions!

- If you notice any of your friends looking a bit shy on their own, go over and have a chat with them to help them feel more confident.

• Help your grown-ups when it's time for food.

• Be a good winner or loser in any party games!

• At the end of your party, thank each of your guests for coming and for any presents they brought and say goodbye.

• And now the tidying up begins!
Groan, groan, I hear you say!!

How to make the invitations

And finally, don't forget to make the invitations.

What you need:

Sheets of A4 card or
paper, cut in half

Pen!

You'll need to include the
following information:

Your friend's name

The date and time of the party

Where the party
is happening

Your grown-up's phone
number so your friends can
let you know if they can come

Any information about the party
theme or what to wear!

Harriet Muncaster

Harriet Muncaster, that's me! I'm the author and illustrator of two young fiction series, Mirabelle and Isadora Moon. I love anything teeny tiny, anything starry, and everything glittery.

Love Mirabelle?
Why not try these too . . .